Versailles Unveiled: Secrets of History's Hidden Enigma

Xanthe Novaire

Published by Novelette Rush Publishing, 2023.

This is a work of fiction. Similarities to real people, places, or events are entirely coincidental.

VERSAILLES UNVEILED: SECRETS OF HISTORY'S HIDDEN ENIGMA

First edition. September 6, 2023.

ISBN: 979-8223686644

Written by Xanthe Novaire.

Also by Xanthe Novaire

Whispers of the Enchanted House: Unraveling Secrets in a Small Town
Seeking Happiness: A Journey of Love and Redemption
Café Amour: A Parisian Love Affair
Versailles Unveiled: Secrets of History's Hidden Enigma

Watch for more at https://books2read.com/Xanthe-Novaire.

Table of Contents

Dedication

To all those who seek to uncover the hidden stories and mysteries of history, this work is dedicated to you. Your curiosity and passion for the past inspire us to delve deeper, to unveil the secrets that have long been concealed. May this dedication ignite your own journey of discovery and transport you to the enchanting world of Versailles.

Prologue: The Dormant Secret of Versailles

In the solemn silence of the Palace of Versailles, where the echoes of revelry and extravagance had long since faded, a dormant secret patiently awaited. It was an enigma intricately woven into the very essence of the palace, a mystery that time had thus far failed to unveil.

The dimly lit corridors, once the stage for hurried footsteps and animated laughter, were now shrouded in a somber penumbra. Majestic portraits of kings and queens gazed steadfastly from the walls, their eyes appearing to track anyone daring to venture forth. The marble floor, once polished to a blinding sheen, now bore the scars of time, small fissures that whispered the tales of centuries past.

At the heart of this palace of faded memories, a solitary figure stood out. He was a guardian, the silent custodian of Versailles' secrets. His weary eyes, furrowed brows, reflected a blend of reverence and trepidation for the place he had long safeguarded.

A gentle breeze whispered through the windows, causing heavy drapes to sway like phantoms of bygone days. The guardian released a profound sigh, as if the murmurs of the walls had penetrated his very soul. "Versailles," he murmured to himself, "holds secrets that should never be consigned to oblivion."

Yet, the shadows of the night also bore hope. Rumors that someone was destined to unravel the dormant mystery began to circulate through the vacant halls. On a silent night, the guardian gazed upon the palace in the faint candlelight, his mind brimming with unanswered questions.

Chapter 1: The Mysterious Invitation

A midst the twilight's shadows, Alex's chamber appeared shrouded in an aura of mystery, with heavy drapes filtering the golden rays of the setting sun. His study, a haven of dusty tomes and ancient scrolls, served as a sanctuary for his relentless pursuit of historical knowledge. Here, amidst shelves brimming with accounts of the past, he dedicated himself to his passion much like an alchemist in quest of the philosopher's stone.

Today, however, something extraordinary awaited Alex. His attention was drawn to the solid oak desk, where an enigmatically fashioned invitation lay. The parchment, aged by the passage of time, exuded an air of antiquity. The delicately etched letters, akin to arabesques framing a secret, read: "Palace of Versailles." The sender, a shadow from the past, set his heart aflutter with curiosity.

He lifted the invitation with fingers that trembled slightly, as though on the verge of unveiling a long-forgotten mystery. Alex's eyes, immersed in their own curiosity, captured every detail of the impeccable calligraphy, and he couldn't help but wonder at the enigma concealed within the Palace of Versailles.

Alex's mind began to weave connections, the tapestry of history unfolding before him. Tales he had heard of lost secrets within the opulent corridors of the palace haunted him.

Whispers of secret passages, hidden chambers, and ancient intrigues echoed in his imagination.

An inner conflict ignited within Alex, a battle between caution and the pursuit of the unknown. His curiosity, that relentless force that had guided him through countless historical discoveries, now flickered like a ravenous flame.

The decision made, he rose from his desk and, with the invitation firmly in hand, approached the window. Outside, night was beginning to enshroud the city in its dark mantle. The moon, a discreet silent witness, shone like an uncertain beacon, casting silver reflections upon the leaves of trees.

The renowned historian, with a determined sigh, had made his choice. He would accept the mysterious invitation and venture into the majestic halls of the Palace of Versailles. With each step towards this journey, Alex was about to unravel the secrets buried beneath layers of history and opulence. His heart brimmed with anticipation, and the unknown stretched before him like a tapestry of intrigues and riddles awaiting unraveling.

Yet, he knew that this decision would lead him into uncharted territory, fraught with challenges and perils. Alex mused to himself, "Versailles, you are an enigma that will finally be deciphered."

As he departed towards the train station, the night wind whispered secrets in Alex's ear, as if the spirits of history were guiding him in his quest. With every step, the future unfolded before him, and the burning curiosity in his chest blazed like an ever-enduring flame. He was ready to plunge into the mystery that now beckoned him with an irresistible allure, determined to unveil what history held within the sumptuous halls of Versailles.

On the station platform, the cold of the night enveloped Alex, causing him to shiver. Yet, this tremor was not solely due to the temperature; it was the expectation, the promise of adventure, and the uncertainty of what he would find in Versailles that made him tremble.

While purchasing his ticket, he overheard a conversation between two fellow travelers nearby. One of them said in a conspiratorial tone, "Have you heard about the historian heading to Versailles? They say he received a mysterious invitation. I think he's searching for lost treasures."

The other replied with a hushed laugh, "Treasures? Ah, my friend, Versailles is a treasure in itself, but there are deeper secrets than you can imagine."

The words of the travelers only fueled Alex's curiosity. The train approached, and he boarded, ready for the journey that would lead him into a world of intrigues and mysteries. As the carriages cut through the night towards Versailles, he contemplated the invitation in his hands and wondered what secrets the grand royal residence held and how he would play his part in the history yet to unfold.

As the train sliced through the night on its way to Versailles, Alex's thoughts drifted through his life, recalling the experiences that had shaped him and transformed him into a passionate historian.

Born in a small town in the heart of France, Alex grew up amidst his grandfather's stories, an old professor who loved sharing tales of the past. It was there, sitting at his grandfather's feet, that his passion for history began to bloom. With each narrative, he found himself transported to distant eras, experiencing epic battles, palace intrigues, and revolutionary scientific discoveries.

Over the years, this passion grew and strengthened. Alex devoured books, from dusty volumes found in libraries to the latest academic publications. His avid mind absorbed every detail, every curiosity, and he became a tireless scholar, dedicated to unraveling the mysteries of the past.

His formal education led him to the University of Paris, where he excelled in his studies of history and archaeology. His professors recognized his exceptional talent and his ability to make surprising connections between seemingly unrelated historical events. Alex began writing articles and academic essays that garnered the attention of the scholarly community.

However, his true journey began when he stumbled upon a collection of ancient scrolls in a forgotten library in the university's depths. Alex's notoriety grew as he published his findings, but it also drew the attention of those who preferred these secrets to remain concealed. He faced threats and intrigues, but his passion for the truth compelled him to persist.

Beyond his academic career, Alex led a quiet personal life. He was single and devoted most of his time to his research and the upkeep of his book-filled study. His modest home reflected his love for history, with antiques and historical artifacts adorning every corner.

In the present moment, as the train carried him to Versailles, Alex felt like a character in one of his own stories. He was about to plunge into a mystery that could rival any of his previous discoveries. As he contemplated the past that had shaped him, he knew he was about to add a new chapter to his own history, a chapter that could change everything.

Chapter 2: An Unexpected Partnership

Alex sat in the carriage that carried him towards the Palace of Versailles. The night had fallen completely, and the city streets were hushed, as if the world held its breath in anticipation of his journey. The historian gazed out the window at the dark landscape, lost in thought.

He knew he was about to enter a world of opulence and extravagance, a world that contrasted starkly with his modest chamber dedicated to historical studies. The palace awaited him as an enigma to be unraveled, and curiosity burned within him like an even fiercer flame.

As the carriage drew nearer to the palace, Alex could see lights shimmering in the majestic halls, and he felt a blend of admiration and restlessness. Everything there was grand, but he knew that beneath the facade of beauty, secrets lay buried within the walls.

The Palace of Versailles, with its majestic grandeur, seemed to embrace the past and the present in a frozen embrace of time. The golden glow of ancient chandeliers sparkled like distant stars, casting dancing shadows on tapestry-lined walls. The air was imbued with the subtle scent of beeswax and history, as if each candle were a beacon of ancient secrets.

Alex, holding the invitation in his hand, entered the royal salons with a discreet reverence for the beauty and mystery that surrounded them. He felt like a solitary traveler in a parallel universe where time had vanished, and stories whispered through the walls.

The rich hues of tapestries blended with the night's shadows, and the marble floor seemed to echo with the silent steps of past explorers. At every corner, a new work of art, a new sculpture, a new story waiting to be revealed.

While exploring an ornate corridor, his eyes were drawn to a figure in the distance. A woman with raven-black hair, elegantly dressed, stood before an oil painting, examining it with a keen gaze. Her name was Sophie, an art historian equally passionate about unraveling the palace's secrets. Much like Alex, her life had been shaped by a passion that had led her into the world of historical discoveries.

Sophie was born into a family of artists in Paris, where creativity and an appreciation for art flowed through her veins from an early age. Her grandfather was a renowned painter, and her mother, a talented sculptor. From childhood, she was immersed in an environment that cherished artistic expression in all its forms.

However, it was during a visit to the Louvre Gallery when Sophie was just seven years old that her passion for art and history truly blossomed. As she gazed upon the masterpieces of famous artists, she felt a deep connection to the past and a burning curiosity to understand the meanings behind the canvases and sculptures.

Sophie studied art history at the University of Paris, where she excelled in deciphering hidden messages within works of art. She could spend hours before a painting, examining every brushstroke and symbolism, often uncovering details that eluded most people.

Her doctoral thesis led her to explore the role of visual arts at the court of Versailles during the reign of Louis XIV. She delved into the history of the palace, studying not only the artworks that adorned its walls but also the artists behind them and the intriguing secrets that might be hidden beneath the court's gilded surface.

Sophie was also a passionate advocate for the preservation of artistic heritage. She worked on projects to restore historical artworks and took part in archaeological expeditions in search of lost artifacts. Her knowledge and dedication made her a respected authority in the field of art history.

But, like Alex, Sophie did not confine herself to the academic world. She believed that true understanding of art and history came from personal experience. She often spent hours in the quiet corridors of the Louvre, absorbing the aura of each artwork and imagining the stories behind them.

When she heard of the mysterious invitation to the Palace of Versailles, Sophie instantly knew it was a unique opportunity. She could not resist the chance to explore the secrets that the royal residence might hold and unveil the mysteries of art that resided there.

In the present, as the train carried her to Versailles, Sophie felt excited and determined. She was about to add a new chapter to her own journey of discovery, a chapter that would merge her passion for art with the quest for historical secrets. With her knowledge and skills, she was prepared to face any challenge that the Palace of Versailles presented on her path.

The gazes of Alex and Sophie met as if they were invisible threads of destiny woven by Versailles itself. A silent recognition passed between them, as if they had shared countless stories in a single glance.

She approached with an enigmatic smile. "You must be Alex," she said in a soft and melodious voice. "I've heard of your arrival."

Alex nodded, impressed by Sophie's elegance and magnetic presence. "And you must be Sophie, the art historian who will share this journey with me."

Sophie nodded. "Exactly. I believe that together, we can unravel the secrets Versailles has held for so long."

As they began to share their discoveries and theories, an unlikely partnership flourished. Their dialogue was a symphony of ideas and knowledge, each word a precious piece of the puzzle they were assembling. They explored the corridors and chambers, delving into the depths of the palace and its history.

Chapter 3: The Secrets of the Royal Quarters

As the days passed, the relationship between Alex and Sophie deepened, evolving from colleagues to friends. They discovered a harmony in their differing approaches to history, a dance of perspectives that enriched their joint quest.

Their daily coexistence in Versailles brought them closer together. The Palace, with its majestic halls and corridors brimming with art and history, became the perfect backdrop for their shared journey. Each time they stood before ancient paintings or historical artifacts, a silent connection was established between them.

Sophie, with her trained eye for art, had the gift of capturing artistic details that would elude untrained eyes. She could discern the nuances in the brushstrokes of a painting and identify the careful choices made by artists centuries ago. With passion and enthusiasm, she shared these discoveries with Alex, revealing hidden layers of meaning behind the artworks.

In turn, Alex enriched Sophie's understanding by providing contextual and historical information. He brought forth the events and personalities that had shaped the period when those artworks were created. His stories and narratives filled the gaps, connecting the dots between art and history, shedding light on the mysteries surrounding Versailles.

They spent hours exploring the nooks and crannies of the palace, engrossed in passionate conversations about the mysteries and intrigues that permeated those centuries-old corridors. Sometimes, as they gazed at a painting, Sophie would whisper to Alex the artistic details she had uncovered, and he would smile, admiring her dedication to art.

At other times, it was Alex who pointed to a historical object and began sharing fascinating stories surrounding it. Sophie listened in awe, his words turning the past into something vivid and tangible.

At night, after a day of exploration and discoveries, they gathered in their temporary accommodations, exchanging ideas and planning their next investigations. Ancient manuscripts and historical documents spread across the table, and the two friends indulged in their passion for unraveling the secrets of Versailles.

Over time, the friendship between Alex and Sophie became an essential part of their journey. They learned to value not only the differences in their approaches but also the richness these differences brought to their research. Together, they danced through history and art, exploring the mysteries of the Palace of Versailles with a bond that only grew stronger with time.

One day, while examining the royal quarters, Sophie noticed something unusual in a portrait of Queen Marie Antoinette. She pointed with enthusiasm to a discreet lever on the frame. Alex, with excitement gleaming in his eyes, pulled the lever, revealing a secret passage that led them to a hidden world beneath the palace.

They exchanged a look filled with anticipation, knowing they had discovered something truly extraordinary. The palace, now more than ever, was a labyrinth of possibilities and enigmas to be unraveled. Alex and Sophie were united by their shared passion and a partnership that promised to reveal the deepest secrets of Versailles.

The royal quarters of Versailles, a stronghold of luxury and history, stretched ahead of Alex and Sophie like an untouched expanse of grandeur. Every step they took echoed through the silent corridors, as if the palace itself were whispering its well-guarded stories.

The faint light of the lanterns they carried danced on the walls, casting undulating shadows over portraits of past monarchs. The paintings seemed to watch them with eyes frozen in time, a silent and eternal audience for their investigations.

Sophie, with a gentle touch, traced the golden frame of a portrait of Queen Marie Antoinette. The figure of the queen was captured in a moment of grace and opulence, but there was something more in her gaze, an undisclosed depth.

"Look at her, Alex," Sophie murmured, her voice tinged with reverence. "Marie Antoinette, an icon and an enigma. What might she have hidden behind that enigmatic gaze?"

Alex, his eyes fixed on the painting, responded with an equally solemn voice: "The curtains of history often conceal dark truths, Sophie. Perhaps this is the moment for us to unveil what lies beyond appearances."

With fervor, they turned to explore the artifacts that adorned the royal chamber. A golden crown, studded with gems that sparkled like distant stars, seemed to pulsate with the heritage of kings. Ancient books, their pages aged by time, exuded the scent of history, containing secrets of the past.

It was while Sophie examined a velvet-upholstered armchair that her hand slipped over a wooden panel. With a sigh of surprise, she revealed a secret drawer, hidden from curious eyes by the passage of time.

Alex and Sophie exchanged expectant looks as the drawer unveiled its treasure: an ancient diary, its yellowed pages filled with handwritten notes, writing that echoed with the voice of centuries past.

As they flipped through the diary, the eyes of Alex and Sophie widened with each revelation. The handwritten words challenged the official version of Versailles' history, hinting at intrigues and conspiracies that could redefine the royal court's past.

Sophie murmured with growing intensity: "This could change everything we know, Alex. These words, these notes, they challenge what we believe to be the truth."

Alex agreed, his thoughts swirling in a whirlwind of emotions and possibilities. "The past has hidden its deep narratives for long enough. Now it is our duty to unearth them, even if they defy historical conventions."

Versailles, with its silent majesty, had revealed yet another of its secrets, and Alex and Sophie were determined to unravel the hidden truth in the shadows of the royal quarters. History was about to be rewritten, and they would be the architects of its new narrative, even if it led them to unknown and perilous territories.

Chapter 4: The Secret Society

The clandestine library resembled a profane temple of knowledge, a sanctuary where ancestral secrets lay concealed among yellowed pages and dusty bookshelves. Candlelight cast dancing shadows on the ancient tomes, transforming the room into a setting of mystery and discovery.

Alex and Sophie traversed the chamber like archaeologists in search of traces from lost civilizations. Each book they opened was a portal to the past, a window to the time when Versailles brimmed with intrigue and conspiracies.

The manuscript that Alex unearthed was a treasure hidden for centuries, its yellowed pages filled with enigmatic symbols and encrypted annotations. Sophie, her eyes gleaming with enthusiasm, drew nearer to examine it more closely.

"It appears to be a record of a secret society intertwined with Versailles," Sophie whispered, her fingers tracing the contours of the illustrations. "A brotherhood that operated in the shadows, stitching its own narrative into the fabric of history."

Alex nodded, his gaze fixed on a symbol that resembled a warning. "But this symbol here, Sophie, a serpent, is like an alert. As if we were on the brink of delving into treacherous waters."

Enthralled by the manuscript, they did not immediately notice the shadowy presence that materialized at the library's entrance. A man dressed in black, with eyes as sharp as daggers, observed them with a cold smile.

"Alex," Sophie murmured, her voice trembling, "there's someone here."

An agent from the rival organization drew closer, his steps as silent as a predator closing in on its prey. His smile, laden with menace, resonated through the bookshelves, filling the air with palpable tension.

"You two are about to entangle yourselves in a web from which you cannot escape," the agent said with calculated malice. "The pursuit of knowledge can exact a high price."

Alex, with fiery determination, responded with a resolute voice: "We fear not the truth, however dark it may be. The secrets of Versailles deserve to be unveiled."

As the shadows of the past stirred around them, they were poised to delve even deeper into the enigma of Versailles, willing to pay any price for answers that could redefine the narrative of history.

Chapter 5: Confrontation in the Library

T he concealed library, once a sanctuary of wisdom, had become the stage for an intellectual clash. There, at the heart of the Palace of Versailles, Alex and Sophie confronted the agent of the rival organization, an enigmatic man dressed in black, whose eyes cut like finely honed daggers.

The atmosphere was heavy, charged with electricity, as if the knowledge accumulated within the pages of dusty books whispered secrets guarded for centuries. The flickering candlelight cast dancing shadows upon the shelves laden with ancient volumes.

Sophie, with her wit as sharp as a masterfully forged blade, took the lead. "Who are you? And why do you attempt to conceal the truth about the secret society of Versailles?"

The rival agent smiled, a smile that seemed to hide more mysteries than revelations. "My name is irrelevant. What matters is that you, with your reckless investigations, are unearthing secrets that should remain hidden."

Alex, his voice unwavering and resolute, countered, "We are not driven by fear but by an insatiable thirst for knowledge and the pursuit of truth. The secret society cannot continue to dwell in anonymity."

The confrontation unfolded like an intricate chess game, where each word was a strategic piece in motion. The rival agent shared enigmatic information and veiled clues, challenging the intelligence and acumen of Alex and Sophie.

Sophie, with astute eyes that captured even the subtlest details, noticed a gap in the agent's words. "You are not a guardian of history but a usurper of Versailles' secrets. Revealing these mysteries threatens the power you hold."

For a moment, the rival agent seemed to falter. A flicker of uncertainty crossed his icy eyes before he regained composure. "We are not the only ones who guard secrets, curious historians. Versailles is a puzzle that only the most fearless can decipher."

The brilliant minds of Alex and Sophie had unveiled part of the veil shrouding the secret society, but the threat from the rival organization persisted, looming like a shadow lurking at the fringes of knowledge. The intellectual conflict was far from over, and the forthcoming revelations could shake the foundations of Versailles and the world beyond its gilded walls. As the words echoed in the concealed library, the fate of Versailles and its custodians hung once again in the balance of history.

Chapter 6: The Enigma of the Gardens

The temporary truce with the rival agent had paved the way for a new chapter in Alex and Sophie's tireless quest for the secrets of Versailles. The gardens, vast and lush, stretched before them like a green carpet woven by nature itself.

As they ventured through the gardens, the rays of the setting sun painted the scene in golden hues, causing the fountains to dance in a ballet of light and shadow. Each step was like a note in a symphony, a melody that guided them toward the unknown.

The palace gardeners watched in silence, their discreet presence adding a layer of mystery to the surroundings. They were silent guardians of the secrets that ancient trees and flower beds could harbor. Each of their glances seemed to whisper, "Exercise caution, for the gardens too have stories to tell."

Alex and Sophie explored the living mazes of carefully trimmed bushes, their steps reverberating like a declaration of determination. Every discovery was a link in the chain that connected them to Versailles' hidden past.

As twilight approached, the scenery transformed into an enchanted nighttime landscape. Twinkling stars dotted the dark sky like diamonds set in black velvet. The silence of the gardens seemed to resonate with the very breath of history itself.

It was then that Alex, illuminating an ancient shrub with a torch, unveiled the secret that awaited them. Within the depths of the shrubbery, an ancient map adorned with mysterious runes and enigmatic symbols revealed itself as a hidden treasure.

Sophie gazed upon the map with eyes gleaming with anticipation. "This map may be the key we were searching for. The secret society has left its mark here, and now we have a concrete lead to unravel its mystery."

Their dialogue was like a melody echoing through the gardens, a harmony of determination and curiosity. The discovery of the map was not just a triumph but an invitation to a new journey, a promise to unravel the riddles awaiting them in the shadows of the past.

Beneath the starry mantle of Versailles' gardens, they were poised to decipher the next chapter of the enigma that had captivated them, determined to follow the clues to the depths of the hidden truths the palace guarded so zealously.

Chapter 7: The Mysterious Map

Night had fallen over Versailles, enveloping the palace in a cloak of shadows and secrets. Alex and Sophie found themselves in their study, where the table had transformed into an altar dedicated to the revelation of ancient mysteries. The map, now spread before them, resembled a portal to the unknown.

The dim candlelight cast golden reflections on the aged parchment, accentuating the intricate symbols that adorned it. Each stroke was a silent sentinel of an ancient narrative, and the room seemed pregnant with promises and mysteries yet to be unraveled.

Determination etched lines of concentration onto Alex's face. His eyes scrutinized the map like an archaeologist unearthing the past, his hands touching the symbols with reverence. "Each symbol, Sophie, is a key to a secret we must unlock. These shapes, these curves, are not random; they are the language of the secret society."

Sophie, with her logical and keen mind, leaned over the map, tracing invisible lines between the symbols. "We need to comprehend what these symbols are telling us. Each one of them could be a link in the chain connecting us to the past, to the truth the secret society wishes to share with us."

The action unfolded like an intellectual dance, with Alex and Sophie delving into the details of the map. Each symbol was decoded, like pieces of a puzzle falling into place. It was a quest for knowledge, a race against time to unveil a secret that had withstood the test of centuries.

Their dialogue was like a symphony of intelligence, a conversation that flowed like the very river of history. Words were exchanged like scrolls revealing secrets, and with each discovery, the tension grew.

The symbols on the map unveiled a clue that would lead them to a new enigma in Versailles' hidden history. The location of the next secret was about to be unveiled, and the suspense was palpable, like an electric charge in the air.

In the candlelit study, Alex and Sophie were ready to embark on a new stage of their journey, determined to follow the map's clues and unravel the mystery the secret society had guarded for so long. With sharpened minds and eager hearts, they were prepared to face whatever the next chapter of their quest would bring. And so, in the shadows of the past, Versailles' history continued to unfold, like an ancient book whose pages revealed ever-deeper secrets.

Chapter 8: The Pursuit of the Enigma

The moon rose majestically in the starry sky, casting its silver mantle over the picturesque surroundings of Versailles. The gardens that surrounded them were a symphony of colors and scents, with night-blooming flowers exuding exotic fragrances that seemed to have been distilled directly from an alchemist's imagination. Shadows danced among the manicured hedges, projecting mysterious shapes that whispered of ancient secrets.

Alex and Sophie were immersed in the nocturnal landscape, shadows dancing around them like specters from the past. The flowerbeds seemed to flash in ephemeral colors, as if the flowers themselves wished to share their wisdom with the nighttime visitors. Every step on the soft ground was like a bow to the history sleeping beneath the gardens of Versailles.

The unfolded map before them now indicated the next enigma that awaited them. Each line and symbol seemed to pulsate with its own energy, as if the ancient parchment were alive. The eyes of Alex and Sophie reflected the urgency of the situation, the gleam of determination mixed with the anxiety of the fierce competition with the rival organization. Each clue followed like an Ariadne's thread, leading them deeper into the mysteries of Versailles but also closer to the approaching threat.

"We are close," Sophie murmured, her French accent adding a touch of charm to the night. She pointed to a small clearing ahead, where an ancient monument stood like a silent guardian of the secrets that lay below the earth.

A local guide, a keeper of the region's ancient knowledge, had joined them in this desperate quest. His name was Étienne, and his knowledge of the trails and hidden secrets around Versailles had become their compass on this journey. His eyes were like lanterns that illuminated the path, revealing details that would go unnoticed by less trained eyes. Every footprint, every mark on the trees, every enigmatic inscription on the rocks was deciphered by Étienne as if they were chapters of an ancient book.

Their footsteps echoed through the silent woods, accompanied by the murmur of streams and the whisper of the wind in the leaves. The atmosphere was laden with an ancient aura, as if Versailles itself was whispering secrets that had been guarded for centuries.

Their dialogue was like an exchange of strategies, an intellectual chess game where each move was calculated with precision. With each revelation, the competition with the rival organization intensified, like an obstacle race where every step had consequences.

"We must be swift," Alex said, his eyes fixed on the map. "The rival organization is not far, and we cannot allow them to arrive first."

Tension hung in the air, like an impending storm. The moon silently witnessed the frenzied search, its silver rays illuminating the uncertain path. The quest for the next enigma was a treasure hunt, but the treasure was not gold or jewels; it was knowledge, the truth that the secret society guarded.

The discovery of the next enigma brought a sigh of relief, but the rival organization was close. The competition was far from over, and the next chapter promised more challenges and twists in the relentless pursuit of the truth hidden in the corridors of the past.

And so, under the watchful eye of the moon and the whisper of the night winds, Alex, Sophie, and their local guide were prepared to face whatever the next enigma brought, determined to unravel the mysteries of Versailles before the rival organization did. The enigma of the night awaited them, and they were ready to decipher it, no matter the cost.

Chapter 9: Subterranean Secrets

The entrance to the underground tunnels was a somber fissure in the earth, akin to the maw of a slumbering behemoth. Alex, Sophie, and Étienne exchanged a determined glance before plunging into the darkness. Their pocket lanterns cast feeble sparks of light upon the damp stone walls, revealing ancient symbols and inscriptions that adorned the narrow passages.

These tunnels were a labyrinth of secrets, a maze concealed for centuries. Each step reverberated in the stifling air, creating a sense of anticipation and unease. The scent of earth and moisture permeated the atmosphere, while the voices from the surface faded, replaced by a profound silence broken only by the echo of their own footsteps.

As they advanced, the tunnel walls unveiled a tapestry of Versailles' history. Paintings and drawings, weathered by time, covered the stone surfaces. Scenes of royal banquets, hunts, and dances seemed to come to life in the lantern light, like ghosts from the past. Alex and Sophie were awed by the art that narrated the palace's history in a way no book ever could.

"This is incredible," Sophie whispered, gently touching one of the faded images.

Étienne nodded, his face illuminated by the lantern's flickering light. "These paintings are the living history of Versailles, hidden deep within the earth."

As they progressed, the tunnels grew narrower and more tortuous, as if guided by an invisible hand. The damp air became denser, and a feeling of oppression surrounded them. Yet, they did not retreat; their desire to unravel the secrets that awaited them was stronger than any discomfort.

The ancient map led them through the twists and turns of the tunnels, revealing secret passages and hidden chambers. Each discovery was a link in a chain of historical events that had been obscured by time and the obscurity of the underground tunnels.

While they explored, their thoughts turned to the secret society that had constructed this intricate labyrinth. Who were these people, and why had they kept these secrets buried so deep? Curiosity transformed into determination, fueling their desire to reach the heart of the mystery.

A stone door rose before them, unveiling a vast and imposing chamber. In the center of the room, a hooded figure awaited them. Their eyes gleamed with a mysterious light, and an enigmatic smile curved their lips.

"Who dares disturb the secrets buried within the bowels of Versailles?" the hooded figure asked in a deep whisper.

Alex exchanged a glance with Sophie and Étienne, aware that they were on the verge of uncovering secrets that would forever change their understanding of Versailles and their own journey. They responded with resolve in their voices as they faced the enigmatic human enigma before them, determined to uncover the truth behind Versailles' subterranean secrets.

Chapter 10: Confrontation in the Depths

The subterranean chamber exuded a dampness that infiltrated the nostrils of Alex and Sophie, leaving them with a sense of oppression. The rough stone walls seemed to close in on them, creating a claustrophobic atmosphere. The sole source of light came from the lanterns held by the hooded members of the secret society, their flames flickering like distant stars in the night sky.

The eyes of the hooded figure gleamed like burning embers in the darkness of the underground chamber. Alex and Sophie found themselves surrounded by members of the secret society, their faces concealed beneath dark cloaks. The silence in the room was palpable, laden with a tension that could be cut with a knife.

"Who are you, and what do you seek?" Alex inquired, his voice resolute despite the anxiety consuming him.

One of the members of the secret society stepped forward, their gravelly voice echoing off the stone walls. "We are the guardians of Versailles' secrets, the keepers of truths forgotten by the world. You have trespassed into our domain in search of answers, and now you must face the consequences."

Sophie glanced at Alex, her eyes conveying a mixture of determination and fear. They knew they were dealing with formidable adversaries, people who had kept the secrets of Versailles' history hidden in the depths of the tunnels for generations.

"We are not your enemies," Sophie stated calmly. "We are here to uncover the truth, to share knowledge with the world. We mean no harm to anyone."

The members of the secret society exchanged silent glances beneath their hoods, as if internally debating the sincerity of Alex and Sophie's words. Finally, the spokesperson of the secret society spoke once more.

"Your thirst for knowledge is evident, but we cannot simply trust your intentions. Before we decide what to do with you, you must prove your determination and wisdom."

The challenge had been set, and Alex and Sophie knew they had no choice but to accept it. They were willing to face any test to continue their quest for the truth. The room lit up with the intensity of their lanterns and sharp minds.

The confrontation in the depths of Versailles' underground tunnels unfolded like a battle of knowledge and strategy. Alex and Sophie answered the secret society members' questions with the knowledge they had gathered on their journey so far. Each response was a startling revelation, a piece of the puzzle that was beginning to fit together.

As the exchange of information continued, an unlikely alliance began to form. The members of the secret society realized that Alex and Sophie were not enemies but allies in their quest for the truth. The tension in the room gradually subsided, replaced by a sense of unity.

Alex and Sophie were captives of the secret society, but not as foes. They now shared a common goal: to reveal the secrets buried in the depths of Versailles and preserve the history that had been forgotten. United, they would face greater challenges and uncover deeper truths than they had ever imagined.

Chapter 11: Hostages of Secrets

In the dimness of the secret chamber, an atmosphere of mystery permeated the surroundings, seeming to reverberate through the stone walls. Lanterns emitting feeble light cast dancing shadows, creating an even more enigmatic ambiance. Alex and Sophie were seated at a sturdy wooden table on one side, while on the other side were the hooded members of the secret society, their features shrouded in darkness.

Minutes stretched into what felt like hours as the tension in the air mounted. Alex and Sophie exchanged a silent agreement: they could not divulge all the secrets they had uncovered thus far. After all, with knowledge came the responsibility to preserve history and protect those who had entrusted their secrets to them.

The leader of the secret society, an imposing figure with a deep voice, broke the silence. "You are in our hands now, and your freedom depends on your willingness to share the knowledge you have diligently sought. What do you know about the secret society and its secrets?"

Alex and Sophie exchanged a determined look before they began to share some of the information they had gathered. They mentioned the clues they had followed, the puzzles they had solved, and the astonishing discoveries they had made about the history of Versailles.

The members of the secret society listened attentively, their gazes hidden beneath their hoods. As the narrative unfolded, a shadow of recognition passed over the concealed faces, revealing that despite their initial reluctance, a mutual understanding was forming.

However, Alex and Sophie did not reveal all the details. They kept the deepest secrets, safeguarding the interests of the history they had sworn to preserve. After all, some things were too precious to be handed over on a silver platter.

The leader of the secret society nodded, apparently satisfied with the provided information. "You have proven your determination to uncover the secrets of Versailles and our willingness to preserve them. Now, the choice is in your hands. Will you continue your quest, knowing that our eyes will be upon you, or will you give up and remain safe?"

Alex and Sophie exchanged looks once more, aware that they faced a difficult choice. But their passion for knowledge and their commitment to preserving history compelled them to continue. They couldn't turn back now, not when they were so close to unraveling the deepest secrets of Versailles.

"We will continue," declared Alex firmly, and Sophie nodded in agreement.

The leader of the secret society inclined their head in approval. "Very well. May your journeys reveal truths worth knowing."

And so, Alex and Sophie remained hostages of the secrets of Versailles, but also dedicated custodians of the history they refused to let fade into oblivion. The choice was made, and their path stretched out before them, filled with challenges and discoveries.

The tension in the room eased somewhat, and the members of the secret society began to reveal themselves, removing the hoods that concealed their faces. Each of them had a story to tell, a connection to Versailles' past and the secrets it held.

Sophie broke the silence, starting a conversation that would be the beginning of an unlikely partnership. "Tell us about the events of 1789 and the French Revolution. How was the secret society involved in those tumultuous events?"

Chapter 12: The Momentous Decision

The secret chamber, nestled deep within the mysterious tunnels of Versailles, stood as a realm of concealed secrets and ancient mystery. Stone walls adorned with ancient inscriptions, bathed only in the flickering light of torches, exuded an aura of untouched history. The symbols etched into the stones told stories of bygone eras, of events that had shaped nations and altered destinies.

In the golden glow of the torchlight, Alex and Sophie found themselves encircled by enigmatic members of the secret society. Each member wore a black cloak shrouding their features, leaving only their gleaming eyes visible. These eyes watched the intruders who had ventured into their subterranean domain with keen scrutiny.

The silence in the secret chamber was palpable, bearing down on the shoulders of all present. Alex and Sophie locked eyes with the members of the secret society, whose gazes were now exposed. Every expression carried a blend of curiosity and anticipation, for all understood that a momentous decision was being made in that very instant.

Sophie, with her soft yet resolute voice, broke the silence. "Our commitment lies with history and the preservation of

Versailles' secrets. We will not divulge all that we know, for it could compromise the integrity of the history we hold dear."

Members of the secret society exchanged glances, and their leader nodded in understanding. "You are trustworthy, young Sophie. We grasp the importance of safeguarding history above all else."

Alex added with determination, "We shall continue our quest for Versailles' secrets, yet remain willing to share relevant and valuable discoveries that can benefit the preservation of history."

The decision was made. Alex and Sophie would not be blind captives of the secrets but responsible guardians of the history they sought to unveil. Members of the secret society nodded in agreement, and a sense of partnership began to take shape among them.

"So be it," declared their leader, "May our mutual pursuit of truth and historical preservation be the foundation of our cooperation."

Members of the secret society retrieved an ancient document from a nearby chest, containing crucial information about the events of 1789 and the French Revolution, as well as the secret society's involvement. Alex and Sophie, now reluctant allies, accepted the document with reverence.

The secret chamber, once heavy with tension, now seemed to overflow with possibilities. A new alliance had been forged, and the fate of Versailles' secrets and that of Alex and Sophie were unexpectedly intertwined.

As they exited the secret chamber, Alex and Sophie knew that even greater challenges awaited them in their quest for knowledge and historical preservation. Yet, they also carried a valuable new connection and the hope that, together, they could unlock Versailles' deepest secrets and protect its history for future generations.

Fate, like the subterranean tunnels of Versailles, was replete with twists and surprises, and Alex and Sophie were prepared for each of them as they continued their journey into the unknown.

Chapter 13: The Price of Truth

The gardens of Versailles, bathed in the soft light of the setting sun, appeared as an oasis of serenity after the tension in the depths of the tunnels. A gentle breeze whispered through the leaves of ancient trees as Alex and Sophie returned to the place where their journey had begun.

They understood that freedom was a delicate gift, for the truth they possessed could shake the very foundations of the secret society. Nevertheless, they also grasped that history deserved preservation, regardless of the consequences.

The members of the secret society, true to their word, had left Alex and Sophie unscathed, yet the threat still loomed over them. The fragile alliance they had forged required vigilance and cunning to safeguard their findings and expose the truth to the world.

As the sun dipped below the horizon, Alex and Sophie sat on a stone bench overlooking the elaborate gardens that stretched before them. Sophie broke the silence, her voice brimming with determination.

"Our journey is far from over, Alex. We have a responsibility to share what we know, but we must also be cautious. The secret society is formidable and will not hesitate to act to protect their secrets."

Alex nodded, his mind already formulating a plan. "I agree, Sophie. We need to find a way to disseminate our research safely, so that the truth reaches the public without us being silenced."

As they discussed strategies beneath the starry sky, the murmurs of the garden seemed to whisper words of encouragement. Every detail of the scene, from the fragrant blooms to the ornate fountains, echoed the spirit of Versailles and its rich history.

Sophie brushed her fingers over the soft petals of a nearby rose, her touch sensing the delicate beauty of nature that contrasted with the shadowy complexity of the secret society. "It's ironic, isn't it, Alex? We've found beauty here, but we've also uncovered the darkest secrets."

Alex looked at her with a determined gaze. "Truth has its price, Sophie. And we are willing to pay it to protect history and justice."

The steps that lay ahead would be challenging, but Alex and Sophie were willing to face the price of truth. They knew they were embroiled in an epic battle between knowledge and silence, and they were determined to emerge victorious.

The night continued to advance, and under the moon's glow, Alex and Sophie devised a plan to expose the secret society and protect the secrets of Versailles. The struggle was far from over, but they were united by a noble purpose, willing to pay any price to preserve the historical truth they had uncovered.

The fate of Versailles' secrets lay in their hands, and beneath the shimmering stars of the gardens, they pledged to fulfill their mission, no matter what the future held.

Chapter 14: Disturbing Revelations

The study of Alex and Sophie, once a sanctuary of knowledge and discovery, was now steeped in the shadow of the unsettling truth they had unearthed. The glow of the candles illuminated ancient scrolls and stacks of documents strewn across the solid wooden desk.

Sophie sat in a plush red velvet armchair, her gaze fixed on a yellowed parchment adorned with ancient and enigmatic inscriptions. Candlelight danced on her face, accentuating the gravity of her features.

Alex stood at the desk, wearing an expression of profound concentration. His nimble fingers flipped through pages of documents, each revealing a piece of the dark puzzle they were assembling.

The silence was oppressive, broken only by the occasional sound of pages being turned. Alex and Sophie were immersed in their research, unearthing obscure secrets about the true nature of the secret society they faced.

Sophie lifted her eyes from the document she was reading and glanced at Alex with a solemn expression. "These revelations are deeply disturbing, Alex. It seems the secret society is involved in activities that go far beyond what we had imagined."

Alex nodded, his face reflecting the same concern. "Indeed, Sophie. They have influence in places we never suspected. Their connections reach the highest echelons of society."

Sophie rose from her seat and began pacing the room, her steps echoing on the wooden floor. "We need to find a way to reveal this information to the world, Alex, but with caution. If the secret society discovers our plans, we'll be in danger."

Alex closed his eyes for a moment, deep in thought. "I agree, Sophie. We must be strategic and find trustworthy allies. The truth is our greatest weapon, but it is also our greatest responsibility."

As they delved deeper into their investigation, the truth unfolded before them like a complex and sinister puzzle. They discovered that the secret society was involved in activities that threatened not only the history of Versailles but also the stability of entire nations.

The ethical dilemma they now faced was overwhelming. How could they use this disturbing information for good without becoming victims of the very conspiracy they were trying to unravel?

Alex and Sophie knew that the disturbing revelations they had uncovered would alter the course of their lives and perhaps even the fate of many others. The study, once a haven of learning, was now an intellectual battleground where they planned the next move in a deadly game of truths and lies.

As night fell outside, the study filled with tension and uncertainty. It was a dark night, but even darker was the truth unfolding before them.

Now, they faced the monumental task of revealing these disturbing truths to the world while protecting themselves from those willing to do anything to keep their secrets hidden.

Chapter 15: Plan in Motion

The night draped Versailles like a mysterious veil, casting a shadow over the city that held the secrets of its own history. The streets lay deserted, but the bright eyes of Alex and Sophie were determined beacons of light, poised to unveil the darkness enshrouding the secret society. The time to act had come.

The nocturnal silence was interrupted solely by the gentle chiming of the city's clock tower bells. Each toll seemed to mark the rhythm of destiny, a constant reminder that time was passing, and the truth needed to be revealed.

The two partners moved with grace and determination, akin to dancers on a dimly lit stage. Every step was calculated, each movement precise, as if they were following a meticulously rehearsed script.

Their contacts, silent shadows, maneuvered through dark alleys and dimly lit lanes, gathering precious information that would unlock the enigma. They were an extension of Alex and Sophie's arms, reaching into the deepest and most secretive corners of the city.

The scenery was diverse, an intriguing blend of locations ranging from dimly lit streets to the shadowy hallways of ancient buildings. Each place had its own atmosphere, its own story to tell.

Coded conversations and information exchanges resembled notes in a secret concerto. Every word, every gesture, held significance. The supporting characters, loyal allies, were skilled musicians in this symphony of secrets.

Yet the journey was far from tranquil. They encountered obstacles that tested their determination. At times, it felt as if the environment itself was conspiring against them, presenting challenges that demanded creativity and courage.

In a moment of tension, Alex and Sophie found themselves in a dark alley. Their gazes met, and their words were charged with emotion. "We are on the verge of unveiling everything," Alex said with determination. Sophie nodded, her eyes brimming with confidence. They were ready to face whatever lay ahead.

The shadows that had operated in darkness for so long were now being challenged. The truth was emerging from the shadows, and the secret society was beginning to feel threatened.

The battle was just beginning, but Alex and Sophie were willing to risk everything to expose the disturbing truth they had uncovered. The fate of Versailles hung in the balance, and the next pages of this story would be written with courage and determination.

Chapter 16: Race Against Time

The clock of history was ticking, its gears turning relentlessly, while Alex and Sophie found themselves at the epicenter of a storm threatening to engulf them. The secret society, like a cunning shadow, counterattacked with fury and determination. It was a race against time, a race for the truth.

Versailles, with its majestic gardens and fairy-tale palaces, was now the battlefield. The mazes of secret corridors and silent halls were silent witnesses to the struggle for the city's destiny. The imposing architecture was the grand backdrop of a hidden plot.

The gardens of Versailles stretched out like a sea of immaculate greenery, but under the moonlight, they took on an aura of mystery. The leaves whispered undisclosed secrets, and the statues seemed to peer through the shadows. The scent of night flowers hung in the air, a sweet perfume contrasting with the bitterness of the situation.

The night wind whispered undisclosed secrets as Alex and Sophie moved with agility and determination. Their footsteps echoed on the deserted streets, like the beats of their hearts, accelerated by fear and urgency. Every dark dead-end alley led them deeper into the labyrinth of conspiracies.

Members of the secret society were elusive shadows, always lurking in the shadows. The streets of Versailles became a chessboard, where every move could be the last. Coded dialogues were exchanged in hurried whispers as they attempted to decipher the final puzzles leading to the truth.

In a moment of tension, Alex and Sophie found themselves cornered in a narrow alley. Members of the secret society approached, their eyes gleaming with a silent threat. Sophie looked at Alex, and the determination in her eyes didn't waver. "We can't give up now," she whispered.

The dialogue between them was laden with emotion, an exchange of words reflecting the courage and determination burning in their hearts. "We'll face this together," Alex replied, his voice firm.

The race against time reached its climax when they finally deciphered the last puzzle. The revelation that unfolded before them would change everything. The truth, like a lantern in the darkness, illuminated the darkest corners of Versailles. It was a discovery that would shake the foundations of the secret society and unveil unimaginable secrets.

It was a battle that would determine not only their fate but also the fate of Versailles and its hidden secrets. The night was a silent witness to their determination, and the world watched as they prepared for the final battle.

Chapter 17: The Revelation of Secrets

The grand hall, with its architecture echoing the golden times of Versailles, was filled with anticipation and tension. Alex and Sophie, standing at the center of the majestic stage, faced an eager audience. In front of them, members of the secret society occupied their chairs, their expressions ranging from feigned confidence to genuine incredulity. The atmosphere was a blend of historical grandeur and the impending weight of revelation.

The room gleamed with opulence. Crystal chandeliers hung from the ceiling, casting an ethereal and shimmering light over everyone present. Ancient paintings adorned the walls, depicting historical events and prominent figures from Versailles' history. In the center of the room, a marble pedestal stood, awaiting the commotion that was approaching.

Alex and Sophie stood side by side before the audience, with Sophie holding an aged, yellowed document, her hands trembling but her determination unwavering. The tension in the air was palpable, a deep silence foreshadowing the definitive moment.

Alex began, his voice resonating through the majestic hall. "Today, we reveal the truth about this secret society and its secrets that have been shrouded in shadows for centuries."

Sophie, her voice unwavering, added: "We have discovered that you manipulated crucial historical events, controlling rulers and crafting entire chapters of history with well-orchestrated lies."

One of the secret society members, now pale-faced, tried to argue. "This cannot be true!"

Another member, visibly shaken, admitted, "Our actions have caused indescribable suffering."

The words continued to flow, and the secrets that emerged were disturbing and shocking. The truth, once hidden in the shadows, rose with brutal clarity. Corruption, betrayal, and intrigue were its pillars, and its actions had left a trail of destruction for centuries.

The implications of these revelations were profound. They cast an unrelenting light on the power the secret society had built, redefining the understanding of Versailles and its history. The members of the secret society, who had once seen themselves as holders of supreme knowledge, now faced the monstrosity of their actions, and their faces displayed disbelief, anger, and, for some, belated remorse.

The audience's reaction was a whirlwind of emotions. Murmurs of shock and exclamations of disbelief reverberated through the hall, like a symphony of voices reflecting the magnitude of the revelation. Some spectators were shocked by the betrayal they had inadvertently supported, others were outraged by the extent of the conspiracy. All oscillated between a desire for justice and fear of the unknown.

It was a moment when Alex and Sophie, with courage and determination, exposed a network of dark secrets that would change not only the history of Versailles but also the destiny of the world and the legacy of this secret society forever.

Chapter 18: The Awakening of Justice

The revelation echoed through Versailles like a resounding thunder, reverberating through the ornate corridors and opulent chambers of the palace. The gleaming marbles, once symbols of luxury and power, now seemed to silently witness the decline of an era. Crystal chandeliers, once illuminated by sumptuous feasts, now cast distorted shadows that danced around those present in the courtroom.

The courtroom, once a gathering place for Versailles' elite, was now filled with common citizens, eager to witness justice being served. Their gazes were fixed on the defendants, whose elegant attire contrasted sharply with the handcuffs they now wore. Murmurs of indignation and repudiation filled the air.

In the aftermath of the revelation, the authorities of Versailles were forced to take action. The secret society was being dismantled, with its members facing imprisonment and public trials. The façade of respectability they had maintained for so long was now in ruins.

Alex and Sophie, with their unwavering courage and tireless determination, became acclaimed public figures. They were seen as heralds of truth, those who had dared to confront the shadows and bring to light the true history of Versailles. Their lives had changed irrevocably, and they knew the journey was not yet over.

In a courtroom filled with anticipation, the leaders of the secret society faced trial. Their once-masked faces of power were now bare before the judgment. Witnesses came from all corners, sharing stories of manipulation, betrayal, and suffering inflicted by the secret society.

At the height of the trial, an imposing figure, one of the leaders of the secret society, finally admitted the gravity of their actions. He declared loudly and clearly, with a semblance of genuine remorse: "I have committed heinous crimes in the name of this society. It is time to face the consequences of our actions."

These words resonated in the hearts of those who witnessed the trial. Justice was being served, and the power that had lurked in the shadows was now crumbling under the weight of truth.

But even with the dismantling of the secret society and the pursuit of justice underway, Alex and Sophie knew their journey had not yet reached its end. There was more to be uncovered, more stories to be told, and more secrets to be revealed. The fate of Versailles and the world they knew had been irrevocably transformed, and they were willing to face the unknown with courage and determination.

Chapter 19: A New Dawn

The past few weeks had been a whirlwind of events for Alex and Sophie. As they stood at the significant spot where their journey had begun, they gazed at the horizon stretching before them. Tall trees swayed gently in the soft afternoon breeze, creating a serene melody that seemed to embrace them.

The golden sun cast its rays upon the picturesque scene, painting it with soft colors and comforting warmth. The lush grass beneath their feet swayed delicately, as if privy to the secrets that had been unveiled. It was as if nature itself celebrated the triumph of truth. The sky stretched out in a deep blue, without a cloud in sight, as if blessing that moment of tranquility.

Alex and Sophie were lost in deep thoughts, reflecting on the consequences of their actions. They knew they had altered the course of Versailles' history and shaken the foundations of the secret society. It was a burden and an honor they carried with pride and humility.

Their dialogue was a silent exchange of glances and subtle gestures. Words were unnecessary at that moment. They shared a profound bond, forged in the struggle against darkness and the relentless pursuit of truth.

Finally, Alex broke the silence with a gentle voice, like a whisper of hope. "Sophie, our lives have changed in ways we could have never imagined. Now that the secret society has been dismantled, what shall we do next?"

Sophie looked at him with determined eyes, reflecting the same spark he had seen in her since the beginning of their journey. "We will continue our research, Alex. There are more secrets to uncover, more stories to be told. Our quest for truth cannot end here."

As the sun set on the horizon, they knew they stood before a new dawn. The future was uncertain, but with every step they took, they were ready to face the mysteries that awaited them. The pursuit of knowledge, justice, and truth would propel them forward, guiding them toward an unknown but promising destiny.

And so, with the hope of a fresh start and the determination to explore uncharted horizons, Alex and Sophie began to chart the course for the next phase of their journey. After all, the quest for truth was an endless journey, a pursuit that would lead them to uncover the deepest secrets of the world around them and perhaps even the secrets within themselves.

And as the day turned into night, the sky filled with sparkling stars, as if the universe itself bore witness to the beginning of a new and thrilling adventure. They stood there, side by side, ready to face whatever destiny had in store for them, together.

Chapter 20: The Legacy of Versailles

The sun rose over Versailles, bathing the historic sites in a golden light that seemed to caress every stone and bush with a touch of magic. It was a new day, a fresh chapter in Alex and Sophie's journey. The gentle sounds of birds beginning to sing echoed through the gardens, like a natural symphony celebrating life and the history that had been unveiled.

Alex and Sophie strolled along the alleys of Versailles, their steps resonating on the time-worn stones. As they explored the historic sites that had played such a pivotal role in their quest for truth, a sense of reverence enveloped them. Each step was a tribute to the secrets they had unraveled, to the mysteries they had unveiled.

The Château de Versailles rose majestically before them, its towers and domes reaching for the sky. It was an imposing reminder of the grandeur and complexity of human history, a history now intricately linked to their own. They knew that this place had witnessed secrets and intrigues spanning centuries, and it had become a part of their own story.

As they walked through corridors adorned with artworks and tapestries, each painting and sculpture seemed to tell a unique tale. They looked at the images representing crucial moments in Versailles' history, viewing them with fresh eyes, now aware of the secrets hidden behind the glorious façade.

In the Hall of Mirrors, they paused before the ornate mirrors lining the walls, reflecting their image infinitely. It was as if the mirrors themselves were whispering secrets, sharing the stories they had witnessed. They locked eyes, sharing a moment of mutual understanding, knowing their lives would never be the same.

Morning turned into afternoon, and they eventually made their way to Versailles' gardens, where nature melded with architecture in sublime harmony. They sat in the shade of a majestic centuries-old tree, gazing at the lakes and fountains that dotted the gardens. The water flowed gently, like the passage of time, and they contemplated what they had achieved.

Sophie broke the silence with words that carried the weight of their journey. "Alex, what we've done here has changed our lives in unimaginable ways. But it has also changed the history of Versailles. How can we preserve this legacy, this truth?"

Alex looked at her with determined eyes, like someone who had found a higher purpose. "Sophie, we will continue our research, write about what we've discovered, and share the truth with the world. Versailles will not only be a place of secrets but also a symbol of courage and perseverance."

And so, under Versailles' radiant sun, Alex and Sophie pledged to preserve the legacy of truth they had unearthed. Their lives were intertwined with the history of that place, and they would be its guardians of memory, the chroniclers of its story.

The day ended with a symbolic farewell to Versailles but also with the promise of a future filled with discoveries and adventures. They walked away from the site, knowing that Versailles' legacy would live on through them, a bright light in the darkness of the unknown.

Chapter 21: New Horizons

The setting sun painted the sky in hues of orange and red, casting its gentle light upon Alex and Sophie. They stood before a significant location, a starting point for their next journey. It was time to bid farewell to Versailles, a farewell filled with meaning but also promise.

Sophie gazed upon the gardens of Versailles, with their lush flowers swaying gently in the breeze as if waving to them. "Versailles will always be a part of us, Alex. Every secret we unraveled, every mystery we explored, it's all intertwined with this place."

Alex agreed, his eyes reflecting the same mix of nostalgia and anticipation. "Versailles has given us a gift, Sophie, the gift of truth. Now it's our responsibility to carry it forward, to unveil new secrets, reveal new mysteries."

They turned to the place before them, a gateway to the unknown. It was a small boat moored by the edge of the lake, waiting for them. Its calm, deep waters seemed to hold countless untold stories, waiting to be explored.

Sophie took Alex's hand, their fingers interlocking like a promise. "We're ready for the next journey, Alex. To face new horizons, unravel new puzzles, and share the truth with the world."

Alex smiled, a smile filled with determination and courage. "Together, Sophie, we will confront the unknown and continue our quest for knowledge. Each day will be a blank page, ready to be filled with our discoveries."

And so, with the sun setting on the horizon and the boat sailing toward an uncertain future, Alex and Sophie embarked on a new journey. The wind whispered secrets in their ears, promising that the pursuit of truth never ends, that there are always new horizons to explore, and that knowledge is an eternal quest that would forever unite them.

As the sun disappeared on the horizon, they looked ahead, ready to face the unknown, confident that the pursuit of knowledge would guide them toward a destination filled with meaning and discoveries.

Epilogue: The Legacy of Truth

Years had passed since Alex and Sophie embarked on their last journey together. They continued to unravel mysteries, unveil secrets, and share knowledge with the world. Their lives were a constant quest for understanding, a relentless exploration of the unknown.

Over this time, the legacy of Versailles grew. The secret of the secret society had been dismantled, but other mysteries emerged to take its place. Alex and Sophie became renowned researchers, known for their passion for truth and their unwavering pursuit of answers.

Versailles remained a place of special significance for them, a constant reminder of where it all began. They often returned to the gardens where their journey had started, where the setting sun still painted the sky with shades of orange and red. It was as if Versailles embraced them, reminding them that the quest for knowledge never had an end.

Their discoveries changed the world. New stories were written, old myths were debunked, and humanity advanced toward a deeper understanding of its own past and its place in the universe. The legacy of Alex and Sophie was an inheritance for future generations, an inspiration to keep exploring, questioning, and seeking the truth.

And, in the end, the sun continued to set on the horizon, promising a new tomorrow full of possibilities and mysteries to unravel. Knowledge was the light that illuminated the path, and Alex and Sophie, united by love and eternal quest, walked together toward the unknown, ready to face the challenges the future held for them.

The legacy of truth continued to shine, a flame that would never extinguish, an endless journey in search of knowledge, understanding, and above all, truth. And so, the story of Alex and Sophie continued, a tale of passion, curiosity, and courage that would echo through time, inspiring all those who seek the light of wisdom.

Don't miss out!

Visit the website below and you can sign up to receive emails whenever Xanthe Novaire publishes a new book. There's no charge and no obligation.

https://books2read.com/r/B-A-FRZY-OGVNC

BOOKS 2 READ

Connecting independent readers to independent writers.

Did you love *Versailles Unveiled: Secrets of History's Hidden Enigma*? Then you should read *Seeking Happiness: A Journey of Love and Redemption*[1] by Xanthe Novaire!

[2]

Seeking Happiness: A Journey of Love and Redemption

AttentionWelcome to a world of mystery, betrayal, and redemption. Get ready to embark on an exciting journey through the pages of this book, where dark secrets emerge from the shadows and intertwine with the lives of captivating characters.

InterestMeet Emily, James, Sarah, and Lily, four friends whose seemingly ordinary lives hide profound mysteries. A

---

1. https://books2read.com/u/3k6a56

2. https://books2read.com/u/3k6a56

tragic accident puts their lives at stake, revealing a web of conspiracy that entangles them in a plot of corruption and organized crime. With each chapter, their stories intertwine, leading them to face challenges that will test their convictions and force them to confront their inner demons.

Unravel the brilliant mind of the leader of a criminal organization, a powerful and influential man whose motivations remain obscure. Follow Emily and Sarah as they seek justice and redemption, while James grapples with the overwhelming guilt of keeping secrets. Lily, a talented hacker, must balance her thirst for justice with the family ties that connect her to the dangerous plot.

DesireEmbark on a journey full of twists and turns, where courage and loyalty are put to the test. This book offers a unique and thrilling experience, filled with detailed descriptions that will transport readers to the vibrant and mysterious settings of the plot. Each masterfully written word invites them to dive into a world of endless possibilities, where good and evil collide in exciting battles.

Feel the connection with the characters, their joys, and pains, their hopes and fears. Witness how their past choices influence their futures and how the search for truth can unravel secrets that threaten to bring down the pillars of society.

ActionDo not miss the opportunity to experience this thrilling story of resilience, friendship, and love. *"Seeking Happiness"* is a book that will leave an indelible mark on your heart, a read that will captivate you from start to finish, compelling you to reflect on the complexity of human nature.

Now, it's time to open this book and embark on a journey that will take you beyond the printed words. Are you prepared to uncover the hidden secrets in the shadows? Then, dive headfirst into this exciting plot, where the truth is darker than you can imagine.

Action! Read *"Seeking Happiness"* and allow yourself to be taken on an adventure that transcends the limits of imagination. Your destiny awaits within the pages of this book, waiting for you to unravel the mysteries and face the challenges that will change your lives forever. Happy reading!

Read more at https://books2read.com/Xanthe-Novaire.

Also by Xanthe Novaire

Whispers of the Enchanted House: Unraveling Secrets in a Small Town
Seeking Happiness: A Journey of Love and Redemption
Café Amour: A Parisian Love Affair
Versailles Unveiled: Secrets of History's Hidden Enigma

Watch for more at https://books2read.com/Xanthe-Novaire.

About the Author

Xanthe Novaire is a renowned writer known for her captivating narratives and profound storytelling. Her works transport readers to vivid landscapes, revealing the complexities of human emotions through richly developed characters. Novaire's literary portfolio spans across genres, offering immersive experiences and a devoted following. Her genuine connection with readers fosters meaningful conversations and a sense of community.

Read more at https://books2read.com/Xanthe-Novaire.

NOVELETTE RUSH PUBLISHING

About the Publisher

"Novelette Rush Publishing" is an innovative company specializing in fast-paced and captivating novelettes. We curate and publish short, engaging narratives from talented emerging authors, offering thrilling literary experiences without compromising on quality. Join us for a compact burst of inspiration and adventure, tailored for the modern reader seeking impactful storytelling in a quick read format.

Milton Keynes UK
Ingram Content Group UK Ltd.
UKHW011304210923
429112UK00001B/37